Pud's round, spiky-haired head loomed up into Jamie's vision. 'Listen, Carrot-Top,' he growled. 'You're holding up all our attacks when you get the ball. Your job is to cross it over to me in the middle as quick as you can. Got it?'

Jamie tried to break loose, but Pud still had a fistful of his shirt and yanked him back. 'I need some shooting practice so if I don't get the ball, I'll have to boot you at goal instead!'

Pud let Jamie go before Mr Jones noticed anything was going on between them, but his message seemed to have hit home. The very next time Jamie received the ball, he looked up straight away, picked out Pud in the penalty area and curled the ball towards him. Nobody could quite believe their eyes.

The centre was so accurate, Pud never had to move. He simply leant back and crashed the ball between the posts . . .

# ROB CHILDS

# THE BIG CHANCE

**Illustrated by Aidan Potts**

**YOUNG CORGI BOOKS**

THE BIG CHANCE
A YOUNG CORGI BOOK : 0 552 52824 2

First publication in Great Britain

PRINTING HISTORY
Young Corgi edition published 1995
Reprinted 1996, 1997, 1998

Set in 14/18pt New Century Schoolbook by
Phoenix Typesetting, Ilkley, West Yorkshire.

Young Corgi Books are published by Transworld Publishers Ltd,
61–63 Uxbridge Road, Ealing, London W5 5SA,
in Australia by Transworld Publishers (Australia) Pty Ltd,
15–25 Helles Avenue, Moorebank, NSW 2170,
and in New Zealand by Transworld Publishers (NZ) Ltd,
3 William Pickering Drive, Albany, Auckland.

Printed and bound in Great Britain by
Cox & Wyman Ltd, Reading, Berkshire.

For all keen footballers –
of any shape or size!

# 1 Un-Friendly!

'You're joking!' Andrew Weston blurted out. 'You can't have lost 2-0 to that lot.'

His younger brother, Chris, sat on the edge of the bed, getting ready for an after-match bath. He nodded sadly. 'Wished I hadn't told you now. I knew you'd only mock.'

'Well, what d'yer expect? I mean, *nobody* loses to *them*!' Andrew cackled. 'When I played for Dane-bridge, we always thrashed 'em.'

'It was only a friendly.'

'So what? A game's a game,' Andrew insisted. 'If you can't beat a team like that, you must be even worse than I thought.'

'Look, just shut up, will you!' Chris snapped. 'It's got nothing to do with you now. You left ages ago – you're ancient history.'

Andrew laughed. 'That must make Grandad prehistoric! Wait till he hears this result. He won't be able to believe it either.'

Chris sighed. He doubted if their grandfather would be surprised at all. He remembered Grandad's warning last week after seeing the school's new soccer squad practise on the village recreation ground.

'You need a goalscorer, m'lad, to stand a chance of winning anything this season. There's nobody on view here who could find the back of the net without a map and compass!'

It looked as though Grandad was right, as usual, Chris admitted to himself. As Danebridge Primary School's goalie and captain, he'd watched helplessly as his team missed chance after chance at the other end. Even Mr Jones, the head-master, reckoned they should have scored at least six!

Andrew broke into his brother's troubled thoughts. 'When's your next game? I'll try and come along. I could do with a good giggle.'

Chris pulled a face. 'You needn't bother. You can come and cheer us on properly when we're chasing the league and cup double!'

'Now I know you're joking,' Andrew grinned. 'It'll be more like relegation for poor old Danebridge this time.'

He left the room chanting, '*Going down . . . going down . . . going down . . .,*' just escaping Chris's dirty sock that smacked into the door behind him.

'Phew!' Chris breathed out. 'That was close.'

He had brushed the ball with his fingertips at full stretch and heard it scrape the post as he lay on the ground. His thin contact had just been enough to turn the shot wide of the goal.

Philip Smith, Danebridge's gangly central defender, outjumped everybody to nod the corner kick away. That wasn't difficult for him. Philip had a head start on boys his own age,

already standing nearly as tall as Mr Jones.

'Great stuff, Phil!' cried Chris. 'Nobody's going to beat you in the air this season.'

Philip smiled. 'They'll have to bring a step-ladder with them if they want to try!'

Philip rarely minded being teased about his height. Whenever he got his long, lanky legs in a tangle and fell over, he'd just stagger back on to his big feet and join in the laughter. At least in football, like basketball, he'd found a game where his pals were often grateful for his extra height – at both ends of the pitch.

Until Chris's save, a header by

Philip against the crossbar had been the nearest either team had come to scoring in this friendly match on Danebridge recky. Since then, though, he'd been too busy in defence to stray upfield again as the visitors piled on the pressure.

Grandad was watching with interest from the back garden wall of his cottage. He chuckled to himself. 'Well, the boys might not score many goals this season, but reckon they won't be letting many in either.'

Five minutes from the end, however, Danebridge did manage to put the ball into the net – their own. It was a cruel goal.

Philip had the bad luck to deflect a shot the opposite way to his goalkeeper's dive, giving Chris no hope. 'Sorry!' he said with a shrug. 'Just me being clumsy again.'

'Forget it,' Chris grunted, fishing the ball out of the netting. 'Not your fault. Could have happened to anyone.'

There was a harsh laugh from behind the goal. 'Old Daddy-Long-Legs is the only one round here who could have stretched far enough to get a touch to the ball.'

'Belt up, Pud!' Chris ordered. 'Just keep out of it.'

David Bakewell's chubby cheeks went red. 'Don't you tell me to belt up, Weston, or I'll sort you out.'

Coming from Pud, it wasn't a threat to be taken lightly, but the goal had put Chris into a bad mood. 'Listen, clear off, will you! Go and annoy somebody else.'

'Ignore him, Chris, you know what Pud's like,' Philip cut in. 'He's just looking to pick a fight.'

Chris tried to focus his mind on the game once more, but it wasn't easy. Bits of mud were being flicked his way to distract him.

The goalkeeper kept glaring round at the smirking boy, who seemed to like nothing more than having the chance to throw his weight around.

And Pud had plenty of weight to spare.

'You wait till tomorrow at school,' Pud called out when both Chris and Philip were again within earshot. 'I'll bang your heads together.'

He slouched off and Philip grinned at Chris. 'Big talk as usual from old Pud. He'll have a job even reaching up to *my* head!'

Chris tried to smile, but he could do without any hassle from Pud. He already had enough problems on the football pitch. To make matters worse, as the final whistle went to signal their second defeat, he saw Andrew coming over the footbridge across the River Dane.

'Oh, that's all I need,' Chris moaned and then had a idea. 'Wonder if I can get away with just saying we scored the only goal of the game?'

# 2 Talent-Spotting

'Well played!' Chris called out. 'That's right, shoot on sight. Have a go. If you don't shoot, you don't score.'

He felt he was beginning to sound like Grandad, coming out with things like that. But at least they had scored a few goals today – even if it was only a lunchtime kick-about on the school playing field.

The attackers needed as much extra practice as they could get. The next shot from one of them was sliced high into the air, the ball dropping back to earth like a stray bomb well wide of its target.

Little, red-haired Jamie Robertson was underneath it. He jumped up from where he'd been lying on the grass, angrily waving his sketchbook. 'Look what your stupid ball's gone and done!' he complained loudly. 'I've got a great dirty mark on my drawing.'

Jamie had only moved into the village during the summer. He was two years younger than most of the footballers and few of them even knew his name. But that didn't stop him refusing to kick their ball back.

'Come and get it yourselves!' he yelled, ready for action, one foot perched on the ball and sketchbook tucked underneath an arm.

One of the players ran towards him. 'Stop messing about, you little

idiot,' he cried, lunging at the football.

But it was no longer there. Jamie had rolled the ball away under his foot and swivelled to one side, shielding it with his own body. The older boy, mocked by his mates, had several frustrated goes at winning it back and then tried to shove Jamie forcefully off the ball.

That didn't work either. Jamie sprinted away and two more players joined in the chase. They finally trapped him against the hedge and the fence. But to everyone's amazement, Jamie suddenly broke free again. He jinked this way and that to escape their tackles and scampered off, the ball still under close control – until he ran into Pud.

David Bakewell had been hanging around by himself near the game, and now made stopping Jamie his business. He wasn't interested in getting the ball. He simply ploughed straight into the little lad instead. Jamie was knocked clean off his feet and felt like he'd run smack into the side of the school building.

'Hey, you great dollop!' he exclaimed. 'What did you do that for?'

Pud saw red. He bent down and picked Jamie up off the floor, sticking his podgy face right up against Jamie's freckles. 'What did you call me, Gingernut?'

'Dollop!' he cried and whacked Pud on the head with his sketchbook.

Pud dropped him in surprise and Jamie took his chance to flee, the ball forgotten. Pud started to give chase,

then realized it was hopeless. Jamie was far too quick for him and Pud pulled up, trying to act cool as if he wasn't really bothered.

'Got your ball back,' he called to the players. 'You want it?'

'Sure,' Chris replied. 'But you didn't have to be so rough. You're twice his size.'

That was the wrong thing to say. Pud was very touchy on that subject. 'OK, you want it, you fetch it!' he yelled.

He swung his right foot back and gave the ball a mighty hoof away from the field towards the school.

CRASH! A classroom window shattered under the fierce impact. As the footballers stared in shock at the force of Pud's kick, a teacher's angry face appeared behind the broken glass.

The game was swiftly abandoned.

'Let's have a look at your picture,' Chris said.

Jamie reluctantly opened his sketchbook. 'Promise you won't laugh?'

'Don't worry,' Chris reassured him. 'It'll be miles better than anything I can do.'

They were sitting in the cloakroom, keeping out of the way for a while of any prowling teachers. Chris had made a point of searching for Jamie after what had happened earlier. He gave a low whistle.

'Hey! That's brill, Jamie. Wish I could draw like that,' he said in praise and then hesitated. 'Er . . . what is it, exactly?'

Jamie screwed up his freckled face. 'It was meant to be the view down towards the river – until your ball came and ruined it.'

'Yeah, sorry about that. But in a way, I'm glad it did really.'

'Oh, thanks.'

'No, I mean, it let me see how good you are at dribbling a ball. We just couldn't get it back off you.'

'Pud did.'

They grinned. 'I think he might have got the red card in a match for a foul like that,' Chris laughed. 'Typical Pud! Did you see that incredible cannonball of his?'

Jamie shook his head. 'I was too busy running away.'

'You were sure quick off the mark,' Chris smiled. 'Reckon you'd make a great little winger. Fancy playing for the school team, do you?'

'Soccer, you mean? Not thought about it,' Jamie said. 'Up in Scotland, where I come from, we always played rugby.'

'Rugby? At your size?'

'Yeah, why not?' Jamie snorted. 'I used to dodge past all those big kids and score loads of tries. Once I get the ball, I keep it and run.'

'I've noticed,' replied Chris. 'So why don't you come to our next practice and show Jonesy what you can do with the ball at your feet?'

Jamie nodded. 'Might just do that. Could be fun,' he agreed, before a slight doubt crossed his mind. 'Does that Pud play too?'

Chris began to laugh. 'Pud! He's too . . .' He suddenly stopped, remembering that crashing power-drive. 'Um . . . not yet,' he answered, lost in thought.

# 3 Sticks and Stones . . .

'You've got to learn to control that temper of yours, David,' Mr Jones said sternly.

David Bakewell looked blankly up at the headmaster. Mr Jones was about the only one in the school who did not call him Pud.

'Are you listening to me? What have you got to say for yourself?'

The boy shrugged, irritating him. 'Well?' Mr Jones insisted.

'They're always calling me names. It makes me mad.'

'What sort of names?'

He was reluctant to answer, looking down at the floor.

'David, this is the second time you've been sent to my office this week,' Mr Jones continued. 'First there was the broken window, and now you've hit a younger pupil.'

'He called me Dollop and Blobby and things like that,' Pud protested. 'And I'm not fat, I'm just big . . .'

'Yes,' the headmaster cut in. 'Bigger and older than Jamie. You're behaving like a bully.'

Pud glanced up quickly from examining the carpet. 'I'm not a bully,' he claimed, close to tears. 'I'm the one who's *being* bullied – by all them out there who keep calling me names.'

Mr Jones sighed. 'So why did Jamie call you such names?'

Pud hesitated. 'Well, he'd done this cartoon picture of me, right, and made me look like a wobbly jelly,' he began. 'So I grabbed it and tore it up . . .'

His voice trailed away and Mr Jones filled the silence. 'And then you thumped him.'

Pud nodded. 'But why is it always me who gets the blame? I didn't start it.'

'But you certainly made sure you finished it, didn't you?' Mr Jones said. 'You keep getting yourself into trouble

through all this fighting, David. What am I going to do with you?'

'Pick me for the soccer team!'

The sheer cheek of the boy stunned the headmaster. 'You want to play for Danebridge?' he gasped. 'I never knew you had any interest in football.'

'Nobody does,' Pud muttered. 'Nobody ever lets me play.'

'Well, I suppose there's no harm in you coming out to join in a practice. It might even let you run off a bit of steam.'

'I can't run very fast,' Pud admitted.

'You don't have to. The ball travels faster than anybody,' the headmaster smiled. 'But at least we know how hard you can kick a ball – I've got a broken window to prove it.'

Mr Jones was pleased to see Pud respond with a grin. 'Let's give it a try,

then. Perhaps if you show the other lads that you can play a bit, they might become more friendly towards you in future.'

The headmaster made sure, however, that Pud didn't see he had his fingers tightly crossed behind his back as he spoke.

'Glad you wanted to come, Pud . . . er, David,' Chris said as the soccer squad made their way down to the recky after school.

'It's OK, I don't mind you calling me Pud,' came the reply. 'Guess I've kinda got used to that nickname.'

'I think we're going to try you out at centre-forward today – we could do with some more weight up in attack.'

As soon as the words were out of his mouth, Chris bit his lip. He realized he could have put that a lot better.

Pud looked at him suspiciously. 'You trying to be funny, Weston?'

'No, no, sorry, David, I mean Pud . . . er . . .' Chris stammered, going red in the face. 'It's just that we need a good striker . . .'

He gave up trying to explain. Everything he said seemed to come out sounding all wrong.

'I'll be a good striker all right,' Pud smirked. 'I'll strike anybody who makes any more stupid comments like that!'

It didn't take long for Pud to leave his mark – on both the goal and on another player's face.

His very first shot slammed against Chris's crossbar, leaving a dark ball print on the vibrating woodwork. He earned praise from Mr Jones for that effort, but then soon afterwards he was sent home in disgrace.

A defender had deliberately barged into Pud and bounced off him to do a well-practised backward roll. 'Hey, Pudding!' he taunted. 'You got a trampoline or something stuffed under that shirt?'

The boy never had the chance to find out. He was too busy using his own shirt to wipe away the blood from his nose.

At the end of the session, Chris went over to talk to Grandad as usual. 'Did you see Pud get sent off for fighting?'

Grandad nodded. 'A pity the lad's got such a short fuse.'

'Just wish that Pud could take a joke like Phil the Flagpole and laugh it off,' Chris sighed. 'You can say anything to the gentle giant and get away with it.'

'Aye, well, everybody's different,' said Grandad. 'And a good team needs all types of players – big giraffes like

Philip and little greyhounds like that Jamie.'

'What kind of an animal is Pud, do you reckon, Grandad?'

'A wild one, that's for sure,' he chuckled and thought for a moment. 'Maybe a bad-tempered camel with a kick like a mule!'

Andrew came up against the greyhound when Jamie joined the brothers and their friends in a game on the recky at the weekend.

'Go on, Jamie, go, go, go!' shouted Chris, throwing the ball out to him near the touchline.

Jamie sped towards the far goal and barely checked his stride until

Andrew's large, menacing shadow fell across him. Suddenly he dipped a shoulder, dummied to go one way and then the other, before whipping the ball beyond Andrew's reach with the outside of his left boot.

The defender was left sitting on his bottom while Jamie went on to tuck the ball past the keeper's dive for another goal.

'OK, OK, that's enough for now,' Andrew announced. 'End of game for a bit, gang. Bring me that can, will you, our kid, I need a drink.'

Chris found the can in the shade of a nearby tree and pulled up the ring to quench his own thirst. 'Jamie made a real monkey out of you there,' he teased.

Andrew snatched the can. 'Rubbish! I'm four years older than him, remember, I wasn't really trying too

hard. Got to go easy on him.'

Chris laughed. 'Come off it, he skinned you. Admit it, he's magic down the wing.'

'He'll do,' Andrew grunted. 'Might win you a few penalties when defenders trip him up. About the only way you'll score this season, judging by those friendlies! When's your first league match, anyway?'

'Next Wednesday, away at Ashford.'

Andrew whistled. 'Good team usually. Is Jamie playing?'

'Think so. The team's announced on Monday.'

'Bet Pud won't be in it,' Andrew laughed. 'Old Jonesy would have a fit if Pud was in a punch-up on the pitch. Mind you, he could always use him as a heavy roller to flatten out any bumps in the goalmouth!'

'Better not let Pud hear you say something like that – he'd go berserk!'

'Not at me, he wouldn't,' Andrew sneered. 'Let him pick on someone his own size.'

'That's half the trouble,' sighed Chris. 'There isn't anybody else his size!'

# 4 Own Goal

Danebridge were struggling.

As the second half kicked off, they were losing 1-0, and they had Chris to thank for not being more goals behind. The captain had already pulled off three excellent saves to keep his side in the game.

Danebridge's attack had seen little of the ball so far. Jamie spent most of the first half standing alone near the touchline, gazing across the pitch at the tall spire of Ashford Church.

He'd half-hoped he might be substituted so that he could go and do a sketch of that instead.

'What's the matter, Jamie?' Chris said to him at the interval. 'You seem in a dream.'

'Sorry, I was just wishing there was a chance to draw.'

'There still is,' Chris said, not realizing what Jamie really meant. 'But we want to *win*, not just draw!'

Chris wondered why Jamie was giggling, but at least he seemed to have woken up. 'C'mon, team,' he called out. 'Give the ball to Jamie more. Let's show 'em what he can do!'

The Ashford full-back had decided that the little freckled winger was not much of a threat. He took every chance to join his side's early attacks in the second half and was out of position when Jamie suddenly received a pass on the half-way line.

Jamie had space to run with the ball at last and he easily beat two other defenders before a third stepped in to rob him. Jamie wasn't too bothered. He felt part of the game now. He wanted the ball again!

The full-back still didn't sense the change in Jamie's mood and neglected his marking duties again. By the time he got back in defence, it was too late. Jamie was already in full flight and up to his tricks with the ball. He dazzled several players with his fancy footwork and when the full-back did appear in his path, Jamie glided past him as if he didn't exist.

'Pass it, Jamie, pass it!' shouted

Mr Jones, adding his voice to the screams of the boy's teammates. But Jamie ignored them all.

Once he had the ball, that was it. Others had to come and try to take it off him – he wasn't going to give it away to anyone, friend or foe. Jamie wove round almost in a circle, beating the same full-back again by poking the ball cheekily between his legs.

In the end, his mazy run came up against the goalkeeper. He dived down at the winger's feet to smother the ball but Jamie whisked it away like a magician. The ball reappeared behind the keeper and Jamie dribbled it right over the line into the goal itself.

He had scored without even shooting. Jamie trundled the ball all the way back to the centre-circle as well, and only there did he finally have to give it up to allow the game to re-start.

Ashford hit back strongly, however, and would have gone in front again, if it hadn't been for Philip. After Chris had done well to block a shot, the ball ran loose and it was chipped cleverly back over his head. Philip, guarding the goal, leapt up high like a salmon and headed the ball over the bar to safety. Nobody else in the team would even have reached it.

The game was locked at one-all, seeming set for a draw, until luck played its part in the final result. After another snaky run by Jamie down the wing, the ball was only half cleared and a snap-shot caught the

Ashford goalie by surprise. He failed to hold on to the ball, pushing it out in front of him. The centre-half, rushing back to help, could not get out of the way and the ball rebounded off his knee and into the net.

The unfortunate own-goal won the match for Danebridge and Philip shook the poor boy's hand after the final whistle. 'Happened to me in a friendly last week,' he consoled him. 'I know how you feel – terrible!'

Mr Jones could only feel relieved. 'A lucky win today,' he said to Grandad. 'I think I nearly scored an own goal, too.'

'How do you mean?'

'By not picking Pud. Could have

cost us the match. Perhaps we do need someone like him in the attack who packs more of a punch!'

'Aye, but not with his fists, eh?' said Grandad, rubbing his chin in thought. 'Leave it to me, I'll try and have a word with him. Pud might well be the only one who can force young Jamie to pass the ball.'

The headmaster laughed. 'You could be right. At this rate, we're going to need two footballs on the pitch each match. One ball for Jamie and one for all the others to play with!'

The leather football stung Chris's hands but he managed to knock it to one side away from the goal.

'Good stop,' came the call from the shooter.

'Thanks, Pud,' Chris grinned. 'Should have clung on, but it was too hot to handle!'

'I only half-hit that one.'

'I hope you're joking,' said the goal-keeper, not sure whether Pud was trying to kid him. 'Otherwise I'll have to swap my goalie gloves for wicket-keeper's.'

Pud laughed. 'I still don't know why you asked me to come and take shots at you.'

'Simple. I needed some practice in goal, and you're about the only one I know who can shoot straight.'

'What about your brother?'

Chris shook his head, glad Andrew wasn't around to hear his answer. 'Nah, he's OK in defence, but rubbish at shooting. I spend all my time fetching the balls that he slices wide.'

'Come off it, I'm not that stupid. What's the real reason?'

Chris gave a little shrug. 'Guess I wanted to see for myself how well you can really shoot. You weren't around at that practice the other day long enough for me to find out.'

'I can score goals,' Pud boasted. 'Just need to be given the chance to prove it.'

'You had it, but you went and smacked our full-back in the face.'

'Shouldn't have cheeked me, should he?' Pud said, flicking the ball up into the air and meeting it on the volley as it dropped.

Chris had been too busy talking

and was rooted to the spot. He could only stand and stare as the ball zoomed underneath the crossbar and finished up in the undergrowth behind the goal.

'Looks like you'll still be fetching balls,' Pud cackled.

'Don't mind this time,' Chris said. 'That was a great shot, Pud, right in the top corner. Unstoppable!'

He jogged off happily, pleased that

his plan was working. Out of the corner of his eye, Chris had noticed Grandad strolling across towards them from the cottage.

'You've got some power in that right boot of yours, young man,' Grandad praised him. 'What's the left like?'

Pud grew cocky. 'Only use it for standing on. Don't need it when my right's like a rocket.'

'Might be OK for windows,' Grandad chuckled. 'But in a real match, defenders won't wait until you switch the ball on to your strong foot. The chance will be gone.'

Pud pulled a face. 'The chance won't come, anyway. Old Jonesy will never pick me.'

'Well, that's where you just might be wrong,' Grandad said as Chris came up to join them. 'Your headmaster knows you could strengthen the Danebridge team this season, but . . .'

Pud interrupted. 'Look, I'm not gonna let people get away with calling me names. I'm gonna stick up for myself and make 'em shut up.'

'Talking of names, I reckon it's about time you started to earn yourself a few good ones instead,' Grandad told him kindly. 'If you can score a goal or two for the team, the other lads at school will soon give you some proper respect.'

'Now I see why you really wanted me here today,' Pud said to Chris with a wink. 'So you and your Grandad could gang up on me.'

Chris smiled. 'So how about it,

Pud? Do you want to play?'

'Sure,' he replied. 'So long as nobody makes fun of me.'

'Doesn't matter – just keep your mind on the game,' Grandad advised him. 'If they see it upsets you, they'll do it all the more.'

Pud grinned. 'OK, you win, Grandad,' he said cheekily. 'Better get to work on the left foot, then, just in case I do get my big chance . . .'

# 5 Make or Break

'This is make or break time, David,'
Mr Jones told Pud at the start of the
practice match. 'This is your last
chance. Understand?'

The boy nodded. He was deter-
mined to prove he could be worth his
place in the school team. He wanted
so much to do well.

The action passed him by at first.
He was slow to move into spaces and
the players were reluctant to give
him the ball, thinking that he'd lose

it. And when he did miss an open goal, hitting a tame shot wide with his left foot, the stifled giggles made his fists clench.

Somehow, he kept his cool and was soon rewarded. The ball landed perfectly on his right foot just inside the penalty area and Chris again felt the full force of one of Pud's master-blasters. He blocked it in self-defence, but Pud collected the rebound and

there was no way Chris was going to survive another pounding from close-range. He much preferred the trek to the undergrowth than broken fingers!

After that, the others began to look at the podgy Pud in a new light. No-one else could make their star goalie dive for cover! The boys realized that he could, in fact, control and pass a ball as well as anyone, and his team-mates all tried to involve Pud more in their moves.

All except Jamie. He never passed to anybody, and certainly not to Pud. Jamie dribbled himself dizzy as usual down the wing, enjoying his own little private game. The ball seemed tied to his boots on a piece of elastic.

After one solo run along the touch-line, Jamie finally lost the ball and fell over. Pud lost something too – his patience. Jamie didn't realize who helped him back on to his feet until it was too late.

Pud's round, spiky-haired head loomed up into Jamie's vision. 'Listen, Carrot-Top,' he growled. 'You're holding up all our attacks when you get the ball. Your job is to cross it over to me in the middle as quick as you can. Got it?'

Jamie tried to break loose, but Pud still had a fistful of his shirt and

yanked him back. 'I need some shoot-ing practice so if I don't get the ball, I'll have to boot you at goal instead!'

Pud let Jamie go before Mr Jones noticed anything was going on between them, but his message seemed to have hit home. The very next time Jamie received the ball, he looked up straight away, picked out Pud in the penalty area and curled the ball towards him. Nobody could quite believe their eyes.

The centre was so accurate, Pud never had to move. He simply leant back and crashed the ball between the posts.

Mr Jones ended the practice by naming the team to play in the first round of the county cup competition.

It was a home match, and to Pud's huge delight, he was chosen as centre-forward.

Chris slapped him on the back. 'Better than breaking windows, eh?'

Pud grinned. 'The only thing I'll be breaking from now on will be the back of the net.'

That promise did not last very long. Keen to get started and make his debut, Pud was ready and changed long before anyone else on the Saturday morning. He was proud to be wearing Danebridge's red and white striped shirt for the first time. It may not have fitted him terribly well, a bit tight and bulging out around the middle, but it still felt good.

The visitors, Woodbank Juniors, from the other side of the county, were late arriving, and the boys emerged noisily from the convoy of cars. Their first sight of the opposition was Pud juggling a football by himself outside the recky's wooden changing hut.

'Hey, look at the roly-poly!' came the jokey comment from one of the players. 'He's wearing a tent.'

'Perhaps he's got the whole team under that top!' cried another.

A mist of rage came down over Pud. Without thinking, he lashed the ball at the hut with such angry power that it splintered and cracked the old, rotting planking. The Woodbank faces turned pale and the players trooped into the hut in silence, gawping open-mouthed at the damage.

Two spectators were equally

impressed. 'I wonder which of them is the poor kid who's got to mark Pud?' Andrew sniggered to Grandad. ''Cos if Pud's in a bad mood, I'm sure glad it's not me!'

'C'mon, up the Reds!' Andrew yelled as Danebridge spilled out from the hut soon afterwards. 'Let Pud the Bulldozer loose on this lot and they won't know what hit them!'

Chris smiled. 'As long as it's not Pud,' he murmured to himself.

As the teams took the field, Mr Jones shared Chris's nervousness and eyed Pud almost as warily as the Woodbank boys. This might be Pud's big chance but, as referee, he knew

he was also taking one himself. There was always the risk that something would happen to make Pud explode.

Danebridge kicked off and straight away, as Pud received the ball, the Woodbank captain charged in at full speed to rob him and start his own side's first attack. 'It's OK, lads,' he called out, loud enough for Pud to hear. 'The fat kid's no bother. Takes him ten minutes to turn round. Just keep the ball away from that right foot of his.'

Pud stayed silent. He simply made a mental note of the captain's number. 'Right, number six,' he promised himself, 'I'll have you later, one way or the other.'

Most of the early drama and excitement, however, took place around Chris's penalty area. Twice he had to move smartly to keep out goalbound shots and a third effort narrowly fizzed over the bar. All of which made the opening goal a surprise to both teams.

Firstly, because it went to Danebridge . . . and secondly, because their so-called goal-scorer became goal-maker.

# 6 Hot-Shot!

'Clear off, Freckle-Face! Jonesy's told *me* to take this corner.'

Jamie had been about to take the right-wing corner kick himself, intending to swing it into the goalmouth with his left foot, until Pud waddled over. 'I've been taking them in practice,' he protested.

'Not well enough,' Pud smirked. 'I can kick it further than you.'

Jamie could not really argue with that. He left the corner to Pud who hoofed the ball, right-footed, across to the far post. It sailed over the heads of all the players, except one. There was Philip, soaring high to meet it firmly with his forehead.

'Goal!' screamed Andrew from nearby. 'What a header!'

Philip was mobbed by his delighted teammates. 'Wow!' he exclaimed. 'Great to score a goal at the right end this time.'

Jamie kept out of the celebrations and was jogging sulkily back to the half-way line by himself until Mr Jones caught up with him. 'Why didn't *you* take that corner like we'd planned?'

The little boy shot a dirty look towards Pud. He didn't need to say anything. The headmaster knew immediately what must have happened and called Pud over. 'I want Jamie to take the corners on that side, left-footed, so don't go bossing him about. You're not the captain.'

'It worked, didn't it?' Pud answered back.

Mr Jones was stumped for a reply. He could hardly tell Pud off further when his change of tactics had just put Danebridge one goal ahead. Their lead, however, did not last long. Within half a minute, Woodbank were

back on level terms, taking advantage of slack marking to slot in the equalizer.

The headmaster was still feeling a bit grumpy over Pud's cheekiness. 'They've gone and thrown it away,' he muttered under his breath. 'Relaxed too much after scoring themselves.'

He knew the same thing happened to many teams and he couldn't really blame the young boys. They were not used to being in front!

As referee, he was not able to say much, though, and was glad to hear Grandad's shout from the touchline. 'C'mon lads, concentrate. Daft goal to give away, that. Mark tightly now, and try to hit back.'

Chris began yelling orders and encouragement from his goal area to make sure the home defence was better organized again. He was too far away to do the same with the attack, but they seemed to be sorting things out between themselves somehow.

With Pud's strength and Jamie's speed added to the forward line, Danebridge now looked a much more dangerous, attacking force. Each of them, in their own different ways, were posing plenty of problems.

Pud's size and jutting elbows made it hard for defenders to get near enough to take the ball off him. And as for Jamie, they almost gave up trying. Nobody could catch or tackle him

on their own, but the winger's bad habit of holding on to the ball too long meant that he could usually be crowded out by sheer numbers.

'C'mon! I was unmarked,' Pud bellowed after Jamie once again lost the ball. 'I'm being starved of passes.'

'Won't do you any harm to go on a diet, Fatso!' came the remark from behind him and Pud whirled round, his puffy cheeks burning with anger.

'You again, number six. Right, you've asked for it . . .'

Mr Jones, fortunately, was in the right place at the right time and stepped in between the two players. 'Forget it, David, remember what I told you,' he warned and then turned to the Woodbank captain. 'I heard your insult. Apologize and shake hands, both of you.'

As the captain offered his hand, Pud took it eagerly and gave it an extra strong squeeze, making his opponent wince. But just before half-time, the number six saw his chance to get even.

Pud received the ball a metre outside the penalty area and as he tried to work it on to his right foot, the captain clattered into him. The foul sent Pud sprawling to the ground, knocking the wind out of his body — the only thing that prevented the hot-blooded Danebridge striker jumping up to seek revenge.

There was no doubt, however, who was going to take the free kick. Several of the Woodbank team began half-heartedly to form a human wall between the ball and the goal, but none were very keen to put themselves into the firing line. They remembered what had happened to the hut!

Pud didn't need a long run-up. He just stepped forward and whacked it as hard as possible. He had taken deliberate aim – not at the goal but at a certain player in the wall. Like the rest, the number six ducked as the missile sped towards them and the wall collapsed like a row of dominoes.

The ball zoomed on to thud against the post and Jamie was the first to react. He slid the rebound into the net past the helpless goalkeeper to give Danebridge an important 2–1 interval lead.

'Well played, everyone,' the headmaster praised them at the short break. 'Mark up and keep it tight in defence, and with a bit of luck, we might be able to score one or two more goals ourselves.'

They did far more than that. They scored three. All of them from David Bakewell as he completed a wonderful second half hat-trick.

The first was the gentlest of tap-ins. Brought into the side for his extra power, this was a goal even Grandad could have scored. The ball squirted to him in a goalmouth scramble and

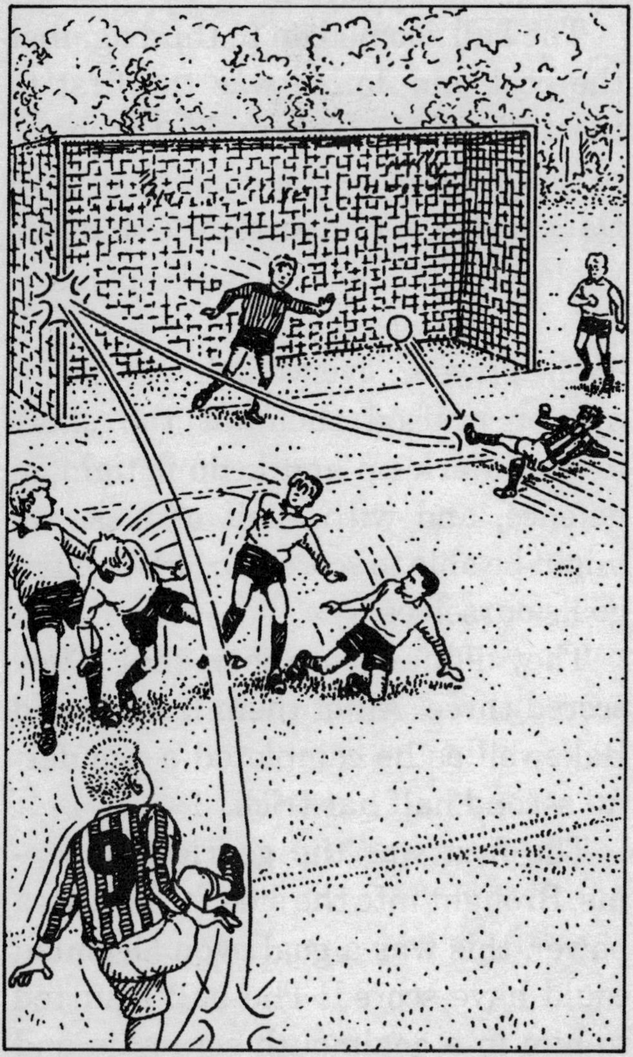

all he had to do was poke it over the line. The thing that pleased him most, however, was that at least it was with his left foot.

The next came as a result of clever work from Jamie down the left wing. He zigzagged in and out of desperate tackles and this time resisted the temptation to show them how it was done all over again. He had seen Pud waving his fist at him. Jamie crossed the ball and Pud's trusty right boot did the rest, hammering his shot wide of the keeper into the far corner of the net.

The visitors seemed to give up now, knowing they were beaten and knocked out of the cup. They could not even bother to taunt Pud any longer. Even the captain had learnt his lesson, still blaming himself for giving away that vital free kick.

Pud was given more freedom and made the most of it, saving his best goal till last. It was a screamer from the edge of the penalty area that made the net bulge out even more than his shirt.

Jamie, amazingly, was one of the first to congratulate Pud on his hat-trick. 'Well done, Big Fellow!' he grinned impishly.

Pud lifted Jamie off the ground in a great bear-hug. 'We make a good double act, you and me, eh? Little and Large!'

It was something of a turning-point for Pud, the first time he'd been able to make a joke against himself like that. The first time also he'd ever been made to feel like a hero by all the other lads. It was a feeling he liked very much indeed!

'Well, well, who'd have believed it, Danebridge scoring five goals in a single match?' the headmaster said to Grandad afterwards as they watched the boys milling around the beaming Pud outside the hut.

Grandad gave his usual chuckle. 'Feared you might have trouble scoring five all season till you discovered Pud and Jamie.'

'With characters like those two around, life will never be dull,' Mr Jones smiled. 'Maybe this season's not going to turn out so badly after all . . .'

**THE END**

# THE BIG PRIZE

## *ROB CHILDS*

*'Huh! Some lucky mascot you're gonna be – Selworth have got no chance this afternoon with you around!*

Everything seems to be going great for Chris Weston. First he wins the prize for being chosen to be the mascot for the local football league club for their next F.A. Cup match. Then he is picked to play in goal for his school team on the morning of the same day.

But then disaster strikes and Chris can hardly walk, let alone run out on to a pitch. Has his luck suddenly changed for the worse? And will he miss his chance of being a mascot?

0 552 52823 4

All Transworld titles are available by post from:

**Book Service By Post, P.O. Box 29,
Douglas, Isle of Man IM99 1BQ**

Credit cards accepted.
Please telephone 01624 675137, fax 01624 670923
or Internet http://www.bookpost.co.uk or e-mail:
bookshop@enterprise.net for details.

**Free postage and packing in the UK.**
Overseas customers allow £1 per book (paperbacks) and £3 per book
(hardbacks).